by Anna Kang  opher Weyant

THAT'S
(NOT) MINE

Hodder
Children's
Books

To our parents for their loving support
and for teaching us how to share.

HODDER CHILDREN'S BOOKS

First published in Great Britain in 2015 by Hodder and Stoughton.
This paperback edition published in 2016.

Originally published by Amazon Publishing.
Used with permission of Pippin Properties, Inc. through Rights People, London.

Text copyright © Anna Kang, 2015
Illustrations copyright © Christopher Weyant, 2015

The moral rights of the author and illustrator have been asserted.

A CIP catalogue record for this book is available from the British Library.

ISBN: 978 1 444 91833 5

10 9 8 7 6 5 4 3 2 1

Printed and bound in China.

Hodder Children's Books
An imprint of
Hachette Children's Group
Part of Hodder and Stoughton
Carmelite House
50 Victoria Embankment
London EC4Y 0DZ

An Hachette UK Company
www.hachette.co.uk

www.hachettechildrens.co.uk

I was sitting in it before.

I'm sitting in it now.

Well, *this* is mine.

OK, just once.